Adapted by Sharon McKay

Illustrated by Stephanie Pyren-Fortel

BALMUR BOOK PUBLISHING

Copyright © 2000 by Balmur Book Publishing

Published in 2000 by Balmur Book Publishing
35 Alvin Avenue, Toronto, Ontario Canada M4T 2A7
Tel. 416-961-7700 Fax (416) 961-7808
Email books@balmur.com

Distributed in Canada by:
General Distribution Services Ltd.
325 Humber College Blvd. Toronto, Ontario M9W 7C3
Tel. (416) 213-1919 Fax (416) 213-1917
Email cservice@genpub.com

Distributed in the United States by:
General Distribution Services Inc.
PMB 128, 4500 Witmer Industrial Estates,
Niagara Falls, New York 14305-1386
Toll-free Tel. 1-800-805-1083 Toll-free Fax 1-800-481-6207
Email gdsinc@genpub.com

04 03 02 01 00 1 2 3 4 5

Canadian Cataloguing in Publication Data

McKay, Sharon E
Timothy Tweedle, the first Christmas elf

ISBN 1-894454-07-3

I. Pyren-Fortel, Stephanie.   II. Title.

PS8575.A2C47 2000   jC813'.6   C00-932357-0
PZ7M34Ti 2000

U.S. Cataloging-in-Publication Data

McKay, Sharon, 1954–
Timothy Tweedle : the first Christmas elf / adapted by Sharon McKay;
illustrated by Stephanie Pyren-Fortel. – 1ˢᵗ ed.
[40] p.: col. ill.; cm.

Summary: Timothy Tweedle becomes the first Christmas elf when he helps Santa save Christmas.
ISBN 1-894454-07-3 (pbk.)
1. Christmas — Fiction. I. Pyren-Fortel, Stephanie, 1950–. II. Title.
[E] 21 2000 CIP AC

web site: timothytweedle.com
Email: timothy@timothytweedle.com

Printed and bound in Canada

Not so very long ago, and not so very far away, thousand-year-old trees grew in a great forest. One tree was so tall that its branches tickled the clouds. At the bottom of this giant, nestled amongst its roots and hidden by moss, was Elf Village.

One snowy day, as Christmas drew near, many of the elves were in their workshop making toys for all the elf children. They didn't notice a little elf, a tiny elf, the teeniest, tiniest elf ever born in Elf Village, peering into the workshop through a frosty pane of glass.

"Timothy!" a voice behind the little elf scolded. "No peeking."

Timothy turned to find Noelle, his very best friend, standing behind him.

"I saw one, Noelle," he told her breathlessly. "I saw a red wagon! It's for me, I just know it!"

Noelle was about to say more about peeking through windows when Snow Goose swooshed through the trees and landed on the soft ground. "Timothy," she huffed, "I must talk to your grandfather right away."

Just then Tobias Tweedle, Timothy's grandfather, the oldest and wisest elf in Elf Village, came out of the forest carrying an armful of firewood.

"What is it, Snow Goose?" Tobias asked, when he saw how upset she was.

"Your friend South Wind has asked me to warn you," she puffed. "North Wind is brewing up a great storm. Prepare quickly, Tobias. There isn't much time." With those words Snow Goose lifted her giant, white wings and soared up into the sky.

Tobias looked grim. "We must sound the alarm, Timothy," he said. "Hurry!"

As the great bell rang, the elves, big and small, dropped what they were doing and ran to see what was happening.

"What is it Tobias?" they cried. "What is wrong?"

"A storm is brewing!" Tobias exclaimed. Even as he spoke, gusts of wind began to blow. Mothers and fathers took hold of their little ones and leaned into it.

"Everyone, run to your homes!" shouted Tobias over the brewing wind. "You larger elves, gather what food and firewood you can along the way. Timothy! Take shelter. Go!" He didn't mean to sound so gruff, for Tobias Tweedle loved his grandson dearly.

"Grandfather, I can gather wood, too," declared Timothy.

"NO!" boomed Tobias. "You are too little. Do as you are told!"

No, no, no! He wasn't too little. He wasn't!

"Come on, Timothy," Noelle tugged at her friend's jacket.

Speechless, Timothy clutched Noelle's hand and the two raced toward her home.

With the angry wind came a downpour of freezing rain that lashed everything in its path. Small trees crashed down on Elf Village. Roofs of little cottages blew away. Even the limbs of the great fir tree cracked and fell to the ground.

When the two friends reached Noelle's cottage, they looked out in terror as the storm battered their beautiful village.

"I must help," said Timothy, "I must." With those words, he ran back into the raging wind.

"Come back, Timothy," Noelle cried. "Come back!"

The wind twirled Timothy around and around, until he was quite dizzy. Where was his cottage? He had lost his way!

"Grandpa?" Timothy called. "Grandpa!" A swirl of wind whisked Timothy up, up, into the frosty air.

"Help!" he screamed. "Grandpa, help!"

The air grew thin as Timothy pitched and tossed, and then, everything went dark.

Timothy slowly opened his eyes.

"Meow." A fat, orange cat glared at Timothy with two yellow eyes. He shrank back in horror.

"Muffin, my little poopsie-woopsie, what have you got there?" shrieked a voice from above.

Oh, no! A Big Person, thought Timothy. Grandpa had warned him about Big People. "Don't wander across the meadows," he always said. "That is the land of the Big People. They are cruel and unthinking. To them we exist only in stories — we are not real. That is how it has always been. That is how we must keep it."

Timothy looked up at the Big Person who stood on a rickety, junk-filled, horse-drawn wagon. She had red lips, saucer eyes, and a tangled mess of hair that looked like a bird's nest. She was the most frightening creature Timothy had ever seen! Even worse, she wasn't alone.

"Snap! Boo! Get over here," she ordered. "Look what the cat dragged in."

"Coming, Flo," her two brothers mumbled as they stumbled forward. Snap was tall and thin as a rail. Boo was short and round — a pickle barrel with a snowball head.

"Looks like an elf!" snorted Flo. She clambered down from the wagon, scooped Timothy up, and dangled him for her brothers to see.

"What'll we do with it?" asked Boo.

"We'll put it on display. People will pay big money to see this little elf. Snap, toss down that old bird cage."

Snap did as he was told. Before Timothy could protest, Flo chucked him into the cage and shut the door. She threw the cage and elf onto the wagon and climbed back up. With a lurch, the horse plodded away, pulling the wagon and all of its occupants farther and farther from Elf Village.

"Grandpa," sobbed Timothy. "Grandpa, where are you?"

Flo was right. Big People did pay big money to peer at a tiny elf. Day in and day out, they stared at Timothy, and Timothy stared right back. He was often cold, tired, and hungry. And all the while Flo, Boo, and Snap got richer and richer.

One night Timothy rattled the bars of his cage as Flo finished counting up her money. "You can't keep me here forever!" he cried.

"Not forever," smirked Flo. "Twenty years ought to do it." Flo reached for Muffin and gave the cat a pat. "Come here, Poopsie. You guard our little treasure while Mama gets her beauty sleep. Nightie-night."

Muffin glared at Timothy, licked his lips, and closed his yellow eyes.

Timothy lay on the straw trying to figure out how to escape. It was then that he had a positively brilliant idea! He took off his jacket, tore it into shreds, stuffed it through the bars near the sleeping cat, and burrowed under the straw. All he had to do now was wait until morning.

Morning came, as mornings always do. Flo woke, stretched, and —
screamed!

"The elf! Where is the elf? It's gone!" Flo opened the door and
peered into Timothy's empty cage. Nothing!

Timothy's shredded jacket lay under Muffin's paws! Muffin had
eaten Timothy!

"You dimwit, nincompoop furball." Flo glared at the cat. "Out!
Go!" And so, Muffin was banished.

A bit of straw moved. Carefully, Timothy peered out from under it
and looked around. NOW! Timothy leaped out of the cage and ran. He
ran, and he ran, and he ran.

Timothy raced up one hill and down another in the deep snow. His teeth chattered through blue lips. His eyelashes froze together. If only he had his jacket. If only he knew the way home. If only . . .

In the distance someone was loading a sleigh pulled by a reindeer. Timothy needed help. But Grandpa had said never to trust a Big Person. What could he do? He'd die if he stayed out in the bitter cold much longer.

"Help," Timothy cried. "Help!"

The Big Person didn't hear. Exhausted, frozen to the core, Timothy stumbled and tumbled into the snow.

"The poor, wee thing. Where did you find him, Nicholas?" asked Mary, as she tucked a pot holder around Timothy's shivering body. He lay in a tin matchbox that had been placed by a crackling fire.

"It was Comet!" whispered Nicholas, nodding to the reindeer who stood at the cottage door. "I was loading wood onto the sleigh when Comet suddenly bolted. I looked to see what had frightened him and found . . ."

Timothy's eyes opened.

"Nicholas! He's alive!" Mary exclaimed.

"Don't be afraid, Little One," Nicholas said gently. "We mean you no harm."

In truth, Timothy wasn't afraid. Something in the eyes of these two Big People told him not to be.

"My name is Timothy Tweedle," he whispered.

"Well, Timothy Tweedle, you are safe now."

Timothy closed his eyes and slept peacefully for a long, long time.

No one noticed two yellow eyes glaring through the window at the sleeping elf.

"Meow," meowed Muffin.

"The cat came back!" announced Boo.

"Shoo, you elf-eating monster," snarled Flo.

Muffin hissed. There, on the ground, lay Timothy's torn jacket. Muffin pounced on it and gave it a shake. With his nose in the air and his paw extended, Muffin pointed toward the great beyond.

"Maybe the elf isn't dead," declared Boo. "Maybe it escaped!"

"The elf is alive? Muffin is pointing the way? Oh, my lovely Muffy-wuffy. Mommy woves you so!" Flo scooped up the cat and squeezed him tight. "Come on, boys. Let's get my elf back."

With Muffin leading the way, Flo, Boo, and Snap drove the wagon up to Nicholas and Mary's cottage. Boo peered through the window. "They're asleep," he whispered.

"Look around," ordered Flo. "Find out if anyone else is here."

Boo and Snap skulked off into the dark. "Over here," they called from the barn. "Look at all the toys! Hundreds of them!"

"Toys? Toys you say?" said Flo. "We could make a fortune with toys. Forget that pesky elf. He's more trouble than he's worth. Load up, boys! We'll take the lot!"

Nicholas, Mary, and Timothy did not hear the commotion in the barn. Neither did the reindeer sleeping in the field that night.

When the sun came up it was Mary's sweet face that Timothy saw first. She passed him a thimbleful of frothy, hot chocolate just as Nicholas came in. "Ho, ho, ho," he chuckled. "It's good to see you back in the land of the living."

With a pin cushion at his back, Timothy sat up in bed and told Nicholas and Mary his story. Mary dabbed her eyes with a hanky. Grandpa was wrong, Timothy thought. There are some kind Big People.

It was as if Nicholas had read his mind. "Now, Timothy," he said, "tell me if there is something I can do for you."

"All I used to want was a red wagon," Timothy answered shyly. "Now all I want is to go home."

The kind old man's eyes twinkled. "Maybe I can help you with both," he said. "Let's go to the barn and see what we can find."

Mary held out a warm little jacket she had sewn for Timothy and bundled him up snugly. "Nicholas makes Christmas toys for boys and girls all over the world," said Mary, as they walked toward the barn.

"Are boys and girls nice?" asked Timothy.

"Ho, ho, ho," Nicholas laughed. "They are every bit as nice as you are."

Nicholas opened the barn door. And there, where hundreds and hundreds of toys had been, stood empty shelves — not a toy in sight.

"Oh dear, and with Christmas only two days away," cried Mary. "The children will be so disappointed. Who could have done this?"

Timothy knew. "Flo, Boo, Snap, and . . ." a shudder ran down his spine, ". . . and MUFFIN! It's all my fault," Timothy sobbed. "They were after me, Nicholas, but they took the toys instead."

"Oh, Timothy," said Mary, "you are not responsible for the behavior of others. It isn't your fault."

"Mary is right," said Nicholas sadly. "Timothy, I'm afraid I can't give you the red wagon, and I cannot surprise all the children on Christmas morning. But I can get you back to your village."

Just then a soft puff of wind blew. "Hello, old friend," said
Nicholas. He smiled when he saw Timothy's astonished face. "South
Wind is a friend to many, Timothy. Come, now. We'll harness Comet to
the sleigh and he will have you home in no time."

Nicholas and Mary helped their little friend up into the sleigh.
Then, waving good-bye, they watched as Timothy and Comet rode
away on South Wind's back.

Could it be? Was it possible?

The elves cheered and cheered as the sleigh gently landed at the base of the giant fir tree. Timothy climbed down and looked around at his once-beautiful village. It lay in ruins. Before he could take it all in, he was surrounded by his friends.

Tobias heard the noise and came running from his cottage. "Timothy!" he cried. Tobias folded his arms around his grandson and held him close. Grateful tears rolled down the old elf's face.

Noelle was there, too, bouncing and dancing. "Oh, Timothy, I knew you'd be back. I missed you so much."

It was a while before Timothy could tell his tale. But tell it he did, starting with Flo, Boo, Snap, and Muffin, and ending with Mary, Nicholas, and the stolen toys.

"And so you see, we must help Nicholas. We must!" Taking a deep breath, Timothy said, "Who will come back with Comet and me?"

"I will, Timothy." Noelle stepped forward.

"I'll come too," said one elf, and then another, and another.

"No!" Tobias stood in front of them and crossed his arms. "We cannot leave the forest — certainly not for Big People. Besides, Timothy, you are too little to go."

"Grandfather, I may be small, but I am not too little." Timothy stood by Comet. "Nicholas and Mary are special. Please, Grandpa. Come with us."

"No." Tobias turned his back as, one by one, the elves climbed into the sleigh.

"Grandfather?" Timothy tried one last time.

"No!" Tobias Tweedle said yet again. He stood silent and alone. The sleigh lifted off and disappeared into the darkening sky.

No lights shone from the cottage windows. In past years, Mary and Nicholas would have worked late, finishing toys and loading the sleigh. Tonight they had gone to bed early, too sad to think about Christmas.

"The workshop is there." Timothy pointed to the barn as soon as they landed. "We don't have much time. Tomorrow is Christmas Eve."

"To work," said the elves, which is exactly what they did.

At sunrise, Mary and Nicholas woke to the sound of tiny hammers and busy clatter coming from the workshop. They hurried out, swung open the barn door, and gasped.

"I came back, Nicholas," laughed Timothy, "and I brought my friends. We made these toys for the children."

Dolls and balls, trains and wagons, puzzles, blocks, kites and bikes, trucks and cars, skipping ropes, wind-up toys of every kind sat on shelves that reached to the roof. Nicholas looked at each one and his smile spread from ear to ear.

"You are all so kind," Mary dabbed at her eyes. "And you must be tired. Come into the house for some hot chocolate."

The elves ate and drank until they thought they might burst. Then Comet appeared at the door.

"What is it Comet?" asked Nicholas. "I haven't forgotten. Come, I have some fresh hay just for you."

Still Comet snorted, and brayed, and stamped his feet. What was he trying to tell them? Timothy looked outside. A horse neighed, a cat meowed . . . NO! Flo, Boo, and Snap were back, and they were stealing the toys — again!

The elves poured out of the cottage and charged the villainous villains. Nicholas commanded his tiny troops, while Mary threatened the wicked threesome with a rolling pin. In minutes they were tied up with skipping ropes and bundled onto the back of their wagon. But what about Muffin?

The cat hissed from under the wagon. "There you are!" Timothy cried, as he lunged at the cat. Muffin leaped up and landed on the old nag's head. As he sank his claws in, the horse reared up. He charged. He bolted! Wearing Muffin as a hat, the old bag of bones galloped into the woods with the cart and its contents bouncing behind him, never to be seen again.

The elves cheered and swung each other around while Nicholas and Mary laughed heartily.

"Oh, my," Mary paused to catch her breath. "Look at the time! Nicholas, it is almost Christmas Eve! Come, you must get ready."

In the blink of an eye, Nicholas was dressed from top to bottom in a red suit. He slipped into his big boots and wrapped a wide belt around his belly.

"Nicholas," said Mary proudly, "you look as handsome as the day we married."

Everything would have been perfect right then except for one thing. Timothy stood apart from everyone, looking sad. He was thinking about his grandfather.

Just then, the tiniest, tinkling sound was heard.

"Listen!" said Noelle. It was faint at first, but the tinkling grew steadily louder. "It's bells!" exclaimed Noelle.

"It's, it's . . ." Before Timothy could say the words, Snow Goose, decked out for Christmas, landed. Tobias Tweedle sat on her back and smiled. His eyes found Timothy. "Can you forgive a stubborn, old elf, Timothy?" he asked.

"Oh, Grandfather," Timothy scrambled up onto Snow Goose's back and embraced Tobias. "I love you."

Nicholas stepped forward and shook Tobias by the hand. "I'm proud to meet you, Mr. Tweedle. You have a very special grandson."

"Thank you, Sir," said Tobias. "I am very proud of Timothy. He has a big heart."

Timothy could hardly believe his ears.

Tobias handed Nicholas a beautiful, red sack. "I, too, have something to contribute to Christmas," he said. "If you fill this sack with toys every Christmas Eve, it will never be empty."

Nicholas laughed a mighty laugh as he climbed into his sleigh. "Comet! Are all the reindeer ready?"

Comet snorted and the team stamped their feet.

"And what about my assistant?" Nicholas looked at Timothy. "Would you come along and help?"

"Grandpa," Timothy turned to Tobias, "may I go?"

With a tear in his eye, Tobias Tweedle nodded. "You may be small, Timothy, but you will never be too little."

"Ho, ho, ho," Nicholas laughed merrily, as he reached down, lifted Timothy up, and placed him safely in his pocket.

"Now you drive safely, Nicholas. No speeding," Mary tucked a rug around her husband's knees.

Nicholas winked and gave the command. "On, Comet!"

A gentle South Wind scooped up the sleigh and, with eight prancing reindeer in the lead, it soared off into a starry, Christmas sky.

ACKNOWLEDGEMENTS

Mary Denneny Corbett has been a writer of stories and poetry all her life. It was out of her love of writing that Timothy Tweedle was born many years ago. He made his début in one of the poems Mary penned for a granddaughter, Katie. That poem, a story told in rhyme, was the genesis for this book. *Timothy Tweedle, The First Christmas Elf* is poised to become a well-loved seasonal classic. At its very heart it is a family treasure passed from grandmother to granddaughter and from mother to son. We take pride in offering it to you, because for all that Timothy has been, he will become so much more if shared with a wider audience. It has been a long journey for the little guy, but Timothy has finally found his home in your home. The efforts of a very talented team of people have gone into the making of this book, but it wouldn't exist without the creative spark of Mary Denneny Corbett.